Elizabeth

THE CAT WHO WENT TO HEAVEN

Illustrated by Lynd Ward

COLLIER BOOKS
Division of Macmillan Publishing Co., Inc.
New York

TO CYRA THOMAS

Once upon a time, far away in Japan, a poor young artist sat alone in his little house, waiting for his dinner. His housekeeper had gone to market, and he sat sighing to think of all the things he wished she would bring home. He expected her to hurry in at any minute, bowing and opening her little basket to show him how wisely she had spent their few pennies. He heard her step, and jumped up. He was very hungry!

But the housekeeper lingered by the door, and the basket stayed shut.

"Come," he cried, "what is in that basket?"

The housekeeper trembled, and held the basket tight in two hands. "It has seemed to me, sir," she said, "that we are very lonely here." Her wrinkled face looked humble and obstinate.

4

"Lonely!" said the artist. "I should think so! How can we have guests when we have nothing to offer them? It is so long since I have tasted rice cakes that I forget what they taste like!" And he sighed again, for he loved rice cakes, and dumplings, and little cakes filled with sweet bean jelly. He loved tea served in fine china cups, in company with some friend, seated on flat cushions, talking perhaps about a spray of peach blossoms standing like a little princess in an alcove. But weeks and weeks had gone by since any one had bought even the smallest picture. The poor artist was glad enough to have rice and a coarse fish now and then. If he did not sell another picture soon, he would not have even that. His eyes went back to the basket. Perhaps the old woman had managed to pick up a turnip or two, or even a peach, too ripe to haggle long over.

"Sir," said the housekeeper, seeing the direction of his look, "it has often seemed to me that I was kept awake by rats."

At that the artist laughed out loud.

"Rats?" he repeated. "Rats? My dear old woman, no rats come to such a poor house as this where not the smallest crumb falls to the mats."

Then he looked at the housekeeper and a dreadful suspicion filled his mind.

"You have brought us home nothing to eat!" he said.

"True, master," said the old woman sorrowfully.

"You have brought us home a cat!" said the artist.

"My master knows everything!" answered the housekeeper, bowing low.

Then the artist jumped to his feet, and strode up and down the room, and pulled his hair, and it seemed to him that he would die of hunger and anger.

"A cat? A cat?" he cried. "Have you gone mad? Here we are starving and you must bring home a goblin, a goblin to share the little we have, and perhaps to suck our blood at night! Yes! it will be fine to wake up in the dark and feel teeth at our throats and look into eyes as big as lanterns! But perhaps you are right! Perhaps we are so miserable it would be a good thing to have us die at once, and be carried over the ridgepoles in the jaws of a devil!"

"But master, master, there are many good cats, too!" cried the poor old woman. "Have you forgotten the little boy who drew all the pictures of cats on the screens of the deserted temple and then went to sleep in a closet and heard such a racket in the middle of the night? And in the morning when he awoke again, he found the giant rat lying dead, master—the rat who had come to kill him! Who destroyed the rat, sir, tell me that? It was his own cats, there they sat on the screen as he had drawn them, but there was blood on their claws! And he became a great artist like yourself. Surely, there are many good cats, master."

Then the old woman began to cry. The artist stopped and looked at her as the tears fell from her bright black eyes and ran down the wrinkles in her cheeks. Why should he be angry? He had gone hungry before.

"Well, well," he said, "sometimes it is good fortune to have even a devil in the household. It keeps other devils away. Now I suppose this cat of yours will wish to eat. Perhaps it may arrange for us to have some food in the house. Who knows? We can't be worse off than we are."

The housekeeper bowed very low in gratitude.

"There is not a kinder heart in the whole town than my master's," she said, and prepared to carry the covered basket into the kitchen.

But the artist stopped her. Like all artists he was curious.

"Let us see the creature," he said, pretending he scarcely cared whether he saw it or not.

So the old woman put down the basket and opened the lid. Nothing happened for a moment. Then a round, pretty, white head came slowly above the bamboo, and two big yellow eyes looked about the room, and a little white paw appeared on the rim. Suddenly, without moving the basket at all, a little white cat jumped out on the mats, and stood there as a person might stand who scarcely knew if she were welcome. Now that the cat was out of the basket, the artist saw that she had yellow and black spots on her sides, a little tail like a rabbit's, and that she did everything daintily.

"Oh, a three-colored cat," said the artist. "Why didn't you say so from the beginning? They are very lucky, I understand."

As soon as the little cat heard him speak so kindly, she walked over to him and bowed down her head as though she were saluting him, while the old woman clapped her hands for joy. The artist forgot that he was hungry. He had seen nothing so lovely as their cat for a long time.

"She will have to have a name," he declared, sitting down again on the old matting while the cat stood sedately before him. "Let me see: she is like new snow dotted with gold pieces and lacquer; she is like a white flower on which butterflies of two kinds have alighted; she is like——"

But here he stopped. For a sound like a teakettle crooning on the fire was filling his little room.

"How contented!" sighed the artist. "This is better than rice." Then he said to the housekeeper, "We have been lonely, I see now."

"May I humbly suggest," said the housekeeper, "that we call this cat Good Fortune?"

Somehow the name reminded the artist of all his troubles.

"Anything will do," he said, getting up and tightening his belt over his empty stomach, "but take her to the kitchen now, out of the way." No sooner were the words out of his mouth than the little cat rose and walked away, softly and meekly.

The First Song of the Housekeeper

I'm poor and I'm old,
My hair has gone gray,
My robe is all patches,
My sash is not gay.

The fat God of Luck
Never enters our door,
And no visitors come
To drink tea any more.

Yet I hold my head high
As I walk through the town.
While I serve such a master
My heart's not bowed down!

The next morning the artist found the cat curled up in a ball on his cushion.

"Ah! the softest place, I see!" said he. Good Fortune immediately rose, and moving away, began to wash herself with the greatest thoroughness and dexterity. When the housekeeper came back from market and cooked the small meal, Good Fortune did not go near the stove, though her eyes wandered toward it now and then and her thistle-down whiskers quivered slightly with hunger. She happened to be present when the old woman brought in a low table and set it before her master. Next came a bowl of fish soup—goodness knows how the housekeeper must have wheedled to get that fish!—but Good Fortune made a point of keeping her eyes in the other direction.

"One would say," said the artist, pleased by her behavior, "that she understood it is not polite to stare at people while they eat. She has been very properly brought up. From whom did you buy her?"

"I bought her from a fisherman in the market," said the

old woman. "She is the eldest daughter of his chief cat. You know a junk never puts out to sea without a cat to frighten away the water devils."

"Pooh!" said the artist. "A cat doesn't frighten devils. They are kin. The sea demons spare a ship out of courtesy to the cat, not from fear of her."

The old woman did not contradict. She knew her place better than that. Good Fortune continued to sit with her face to the wall.

The artist took another sip or two of soup. Then he said to the housekeeper, "Please be kind enough to bring a bowl for Good Fortune when you bring my rice. She must be hungry."

When the bowl came he called her politely. Having been properly invited, Good Fortune stopped looking at the other side of the room, and came to sit beside her master. She took care not to eat hurriedly and soil her white round chin. Although she must have been very hungry, she would eat only half her rice. It was as though she kept the rest for the next day, wishing to be no more of a burden than she could help.

So the days went. Each morning the artist knelt quietly on a mat and painted beautiful little pictures that no one bought: some of warriors with two swords; some of lovely ladies doing up their long curtains of hair; some of the demons of the wind blowing out their cheeks; and some little laughable ones of rabbits running in the moonlight, or fat badgers beating on their stomachs like drums. While he worked, the old woman went to market with a few of their remaining pennies; she spent the rest of her time in cooking, washing, scrubbing, and darning to keep their threadbare house and their threadbare clothes together. Good Fortune, having found that she was unable to help either of them, sat quietly in the sun, ate as little as she could, and often spent hours with lowered head before the image of the Buddha on its low shelf.

"She is praying to the Enlightened One," said the housekeeper in admiration.

"She is catching flies," said the artist. "You would believe anything wonderful of your spotted cat." Perhaps he was a little ashamed to remember how seldom he prayed now when his heart felt so heavy.

But one day he was forced to admit that Good Fortune was not like other cats. He was sitting in his especial room watching sparrows fly in and out of the hydrangea bushes outside, when he saw Good Fortune leap from a shadow and catch a bird. In a second the brown wings, the black-capped head, the legs like briers, the frightened eyes, were between her paws. The artist would have clapped his hands and tried to scare her away, but before he had time to make the least move, he saw Good Fortune hesitate and then slowly, slowly, lift first one white paw and then another from the sparrow. Unhurt, in a loud whir of wings, the bird flew away.

"What mercy!" cried the artist, and the tears came into his eyes. Well he knew his cat must be hungry and well he knew what hunger felt like. "I am ashamed when I think that I called such a cat a goblin," he thought. "Why, she is more virtuous than a priest."

It was just then, at that very moment, that the old housekeeper appeared, trying hard to hide her excitement.

"Master!" she said as soon as she could find words.

"Master! The head priest from the temple himself is here in the next room and wishes to see you. What, oh what, do you think His Honor has come here for?"

"The priest from the temple wishes to see me?" repeated the artist, scarcely able to believe his ears, for the priest was a very important person, not one likely to spend his time in visiting poor artists whom nobody thought much of. When the housekeeper had nodded her head until it nearly fell off, the artist felt as excited as she did. But he forced himself to be calm.

"Run! run!" he exclaimed. "Buy tea and cakes," and he pressed into the old woman's hands the last thing of value he owned, the vase which stood in the alcove of his room and always held a branch or spray of flowers. But even if his room must be bare after this, the artist did not hesitate: no guest could be turned away without proper entertainment. He was ashamed to think that he had kept the priest waiting for even a minute and had not seen him coming and welcomed him at the door. He scarcely felt Good Fortune rub encouragingly against his ankles as he hurried off.

In the next room the priest sat, lost in meditation. The artist bowed low before him, drawing in his breath politely, and then waited to be noticed. It seemed to him a century before the priest lifted his head and the far-off look went out of his eyes. Then the artist bowed again and said that his house was honored forever by so holy a presence.

The priest wasted no time in coming to the point.

"We desire," said he, "a painting of the death of our Lord Buddha for the temple. There was some discussion as to the artist, so we put slips of paper, each marked with a name, before the central image in the great hall, and in the morning all the slips had blown away but yours. So we knew Buddha's will in the matter. Hearing something of your circumstances, I have brought a first payment with me so that you may relieve your mind of worry while at your work. Only a clear pool has beautiful reflections. If the work is successful, as we hope, your fortune is made, for what the temple approves becomes the fashion in the town." With that the priest drew a heavy purse from his belt.

The artist never remembered how he thanked the priest, or served him the ceremonial tea, or bowed him to his narrow gate. Here at last was a chance for fame and fortune. He felt that this might be all a dream. Why had the Buddha chosen him? He had been too sad to pray often and the housekeeper too busy—could it be that Buddha would listen to the prayers of a little spotted cat? He was afraid that he would wake up and find that the whole thing was an apparition and that the purse was filled with withered leaves. Perhaps he never would have come to himself if he had not been roused by a very curious noise.

It was a double kind of noise. It was not exactly like any noise that the artist had ever heard. The artist, who was always curious, went into the kitchen to see what could be making the sound, and there, sure enough, were the housekeeper and Good Fortune, and one was crying for joy and one was purring for joy, and it would have been hard to have said which was making more noise. At that the artist had to laugh out loud, but it was not his old sad sort of laugh, this was like a boy's—and he took them both into his arms. Then there were three sounds of joy in the poor old kitchen.

The Second Song of the Housekeeper

Now let me laugh and let me cry
With happiness, to know at last
I'll see him famous e'er I die
With all his poverty in the past!
I'll see the sand of the garden walk
Marked with the footprints of the great,
And noblemen shall stand and talk
At ease about my master's gate!

Early the next morning, before the sun was up, the housekeeper rose and cleaned the house. She swept and scrubbed until the mats looked like worn silver and the wood shone like pale gold. Then she hurried to market and purchased a spray of flowers to put in the vase, which she had of course bought back the night before with the first money from the priest's purse. In the meantime the artist dressed himself carefully in his holiday clothes, combed his hair until it shone like lacquer, and then went to pray before the shelf of the Buddha. There sat Good Fortune already, looking very earnest, but she moved over the moment she saw her master. Together they sat before the image, the artist raising his hands and striking them softly from time to time to call attention to his prayers. Then, with a final low bow, he went into the next room and sat formally on his mat. He had never felt more excited and happy in his life.

Today he was to begin his painting of the death of Buddha to be hung in the village temple and seen perhaps by the children of his children's children. The honor of it almost overcame him. But he sat upright and expressionless, looking before him like a samurai knight receiving the instructions of his master. There were no rolls of silk near him, no cakes of ink with raised patterns of flowers on their tops, no beautiful brushes, nor jar of fresh spring water. He must strive to understand the Buddha before he could paint him.

First he thought of the Buddha as Siddhartha, the young Indian prince. And the artist imagined that his poor small room was a great chamber and that there were columns of gilded wood holding up a high ceiling above him. He imagined that he heard water falling from perfumed fountains near by. He imagined that young warriors stood grouped about him, gay and witty boys listening with him to a girl playing on a long instrument shaped like a peacock with a tail of peacock feathers. He imagined that his poor hydrangeas were a forest of fruit trees and palms leading down to pools filled with pink and white lotuses, and that the sparrows he knew so well were white swans flying across the sky.

When the horse of a passing farmer whinnied, he thought he heard war horses neighing in their stables and the trumpeting of an elephant, and that soon he would go out to compete with the other princes for the hand of his bride, drawing the bow no other man could draw, riding the horse no other man could ride, hewing down with his sword two trees where the others hewed down but one, and so winning his princess, Yosadhara, amid the applause of all the world.

Even in that moment of triumph, the artist knew that Siddhartha felt no shadow of ill will toward his rivals. He was all fire and gentleness. A smile curved his lips. He held his head high like a stag walking in a dewy meadow. The artist looked about among his imaginary companions. All were young, all were beautiful. They had but to ask a boon and Siddhartha's heart was reaching out to grant it before the words could be spoken. The swans flew over his gardens and feared no arrow. The deer stared unafraid from thickets of flowers.

The artist sat in his poor worn clothes on his thin cushion and felt silks against his skin. Heavy earrings weighed down his ears. A rope of pearls and emeralds swung at his throat. When his old housekeeper brought in his simple midday meal, he imagined that a train of servants had entered, carrying golden dishes heaped with the rarest food. When Good Fortune came in, cautiously putting one paw before the other, he imagined that a dancing girl had come to entertain him, walking in golden sandals.

"Welcome, thrice welcome!" he cried to her. But apparently Good Fortune had thought the room was empty, for she nearly jumped out of her skin when she heard him speak, and ran away with her white button of a tail in the air.

"How wrong of you to disturb the master!" scolded the housekeeper. But the artist was not disturbed. He was still Prince Siddhartha and he was still wondering if all the world could be as happy as those who lived within the vine-covered walls of the palace which the king his father had given him.

The second day began like the first. The housekeeper rose before dawn and although there was not a smudge of dirt or a speck of dust anywhere in the house, she washed and swept and rubbed and polished as before. Then she hurried to the market early to buy a new spray of flowers. The artist got up early, too, and made himself as worthy as possible of reflecting upon the Buddha. And once more when he went to pray, there was Good Fortune, shining like a narcissus, and gold as a narcissus' heart, and black as a beetle on a narcissus petal, sitting quietly before the shelf where sat the household image of the Buddha. No sooner did she see the artist than she jumped to her feet, lowered her head as though she were bowing, and moved over to make room for him. They meditated as before, the artist occasionally striking his hand softly, and the cat sitting very still and proper with her paws side by side.

Then the artist went into his room beside the hydrangeas. Today he reflected upon the renunciation of Siddhartha. Again he was the prince, but now he ordered his chariot and for the first time drove unannounced through the city. He saw an old man, and a man sick with fever and a dead man. He looked at his bracelets—but gold could do no good to such as these. He, the prince of the land, was at last helpless to help.

The head of the artist hung heavy on his breast. He thought he smelled a garland of flowers, but the sweetness

19

sickened him. They brought word that a son had been born to him, but he only thought how sad life would be for the child. When the housekeeper came with rice, he sent her away without tasting it, and when Good Fortune wandered in with big watchful eyes, he told her that he was in no mood for entertainment. Evening drew closer, but still the artist did not stir. The housekeeper looked in, but went away again. Good Fortune mewed anxiously, but the artist did not hear her.

For now the artist imagined that Prince Siddhartha had secretly sent for his chariot driver and Kanthaka, his white horse. He had gazed long at his sleeping wife and the little baby she held in her arms. Now he was in the darkness of his garden; now he rode quietly through the sleeping city; now he was galloping down the long roads that shone pale and light in the darkness; and now he was in the forest and had come to the end of his father's kingdom. Siddhartha has cut off his long hair. He has taken off his princely garments. He has hung his sword to white Kanthaka's saddle. Let Channa take them back to the palace. It is not with them that he can save the world from its suffering.

So intensely had the artist lived through the pain of the prince in his hour of giving up all the beautiful world of his youth, that next morning he was very, very tired. But when he heard the housekeeper polishing and rubbing and sweeping and scrubbing again, he, too, rose and dressed in his poor best and sat beside Good Fortune, praying before the image of the Buddha.

Then he went to the room that overlooked the hydrangea bushes and the sparrows and again he sat on his mat. Again he imagined that he was Siddhartha. But now he imagined that for years he had wandered on foot, begging for his food and seeking wisdom. At last he sat in a forest under a bo tree and the devils came and tempted him with sights terrible and sights beautiful. Just before dawn, it seemed to him that a great wisdom came to him and he understood why people suffer and also how they can in other lives escape their sufferings. With this knowledge he became the Enlightened One, the Buddha.

Now the artist felt a great peace come over him, and a love for all the world that flowed out even to the smallest grains of sand on the furthest beaches. As he had felt for his wife and little son, he now felt for everything that lived and moved, and even for the trees and mosses, the rocks and stones and the waves, which some day he believed would in their turn be men and suffer and be happy as men are.

When the housekeeper and Good Fortune came with his food, he thought his first disciples had come to him, and he taught them of the Way they should follow. He felt himself growing old in teaching and carrying happiness through the land. When he was eighty, he knew he was near death, and he saw the skies open and all the Hindu gods of the heavens, and of the trees, and the mountains, with his disciples, and the animals of the earth came to bid him farewell.

"But where is the cat?" thought the artist to himself, for even in his vision he remembered that in none of the paintings he had ever seen of the death of Buddha, was a cat represented among the other animals.

"Ah, the cat refused homage to Buddha," he remembered, "and so by her own independent act, only the cat has the doors of Paradise closed in her face."

Thinking of little Good Fortune, the artist felt a sense of sadness before he submerged himself again into the great pool of the peace of Buddha. But, poor man, he was tired to death. In three days he had tried to live a whole marvelous life in his mind. Yet now at least he understood that the Buddha he painted must have the look of one who has been gently brought up and unquestioningly obeyed (that he learned from the first day); and he must have the look of one who has suffered greatly and sacrificed himself (that he learned from the second day); and he must have the look of one who has found peace and given it to others (that he learned on the last day).

So, knowing at last how the Buddha must look, the artist fell asleep and slept for twenty-four hours as though he were dead, while the housekeeper held her breath and the little cat walked on the tips of her white paws. At the end of twenty-four hours, the artist awoke, and calling hastily for brushes, ink, spring water, and a great roll of silk, he drew at one end the figure of the great Buddha reclining upon a couch, his face filled with peace. The artist worked as though he saw the whole scene before his eyes. It had taken him three days to know how the Buddha should look, but it took him less than three hours to paint him to the last fold of his garments, while the housekeeper and Good Fortune looked on with the greatest respect and admiration.

The Third Song of the Housekeeper

Hush, Broom! pray be silent, as a spider at your tasks.
Pot! boil softly, that is all a poor old woman asks.
Birds, sing softly! Winds, go slowly! Noises of the street,
Halt in awe and be ashamed to near my master's feet!
Holy thoughts are in his mind, heavenly desire,
While I boil his chestnuts, here on my little fire.

In the following days the artist painted the various gods of the earth and sky and the disciples who came to say farewell to the Buddha. Sometimes the painting came easy, sometimes it came hard; sometimes the artist was pleased with what he had done, sometimes he was disgusted. He would have grown very thin, if the old woman hadn't coaxed him early and late, now with a little bowl of soup, now with a hot dumpling. Good Fortune went softly about the house, quivering with excitement. She, too, had plenty to eat these days. Her coat shone like silk. Her little whiskers glistened. Whenever the housekeeper's back was turned, she darted in to watch the artist and his mysterious paints and brushes.

"It worries me, sir," said the old housekeeper, when she found the cat tucked behind the artist's sleeve for the twentieth time that day. "She doesn't seem like a cat. She doesn't try to play with the brushes, that I could understand. At night all the things come back to me that you said when I brought her home in the bamboo basket. If she should turn out to be bad and hurt your picture, I should not wish to live."

The artist shook his head. A new idea had come to him and he was too busy to talk.

"Good Fortune will do no harm," he murmured before he forgot about them all, the old woman, the little cat, and even his own hand that held the brushes.

"I hope so, indeed," said the housekeeper anxiously. She picked up Good Fortune, who now wore about her neck a flowered bib on a scarlet silk cord, and looked like a cat of importance. It was at least half an hour before Good Fortune was able to get out of the kitchen. She found her master still lost in contemplation, and sat behind him like a light spot in his shadow. The artist, having finished gods and men, was about to draw the animals who had come to bid farewell to the Buddha before he died. He was considering which animal ought to come first—perhaps the great white elephant which is the largest of beasts, and a symbol of the Buddha; perhaps the horse that served him; or the lion, since his followers sometimes called him the lion of his race. Then the artist thought of how the Buddha loved humble things and he remembered a story.

Once the Buddha was sitting in contemplation under a tree, screened by its leaves from the fierce sunshine. As he sat, hour after hour, the shadow of the tree moved gradually from him and left him with the sunlight like fire beating down on his shaved head. The Buddha, who was considering great matters, never noticed, but the snails saw and were anxious lest harm should come to the master. They crawled from their cool shadows, and assembled in a damp crown upon his head, guarding him with their own bodies until the sun sank and withdrew its rays.

The artist thought, "The snail was the first creature to sacrifice himself for the Buddha. It is fitting he should be shown first in the painting."

So, after thinking about the snails he had seen on walks, their round shell houses, and their little horns, their bodies like some pale-colored wet leaf, and their shy, well-meaning lives, he dipped a brush in spring water, touched it with ink, and drew a snail.

Good Fortune came out of the artist's shadow to look at it. Her whiskers bristled and she put up one paw as though to pat it, and then looked at the artist.

"I am only playing, master," she seemed to say, "but that is a very snail-like snail."

Next the artist sat on his mat and considered the elephant. He thought of his great size and strength and of his wisdom. He himself had never seen an elephant, but he had seen pictures of them painted long ago by Chinese artists, and now he thought of a large white animal, very majestic, with small, kind eyes and long ears lined with pink. He remembered that the elephant was very sacred, having been a symbol of royalty in India. He thought of how Buddha's

mother had dreamed of an elephant before her baby was born.

Then he thought of stranger things. For before Buddha came to earth as Prince Siddhartha, he came, his followers believe, in all sorts of forms, always practicing mercy and teaching those around him. The artist remembered one tale of how the Buddha had been born as a great elephant, living on a range of mountains overlooking a desert. A lake starred with lotuses furnished his drink, and trees bent over him with their branches heavy with fruit. But one day from his high meadows he saw in the desert a large group of men. They moved slowly. Often one fell and the others stopped to lift him once more to his feet. A faint sound of wailing and despair reached his ears. The great elephant was filled with pity. He went out into the burning sands of the desert to meet them.

To the travelers he must have seemed one more terrible apparition, but he spoke to them kindly in a human voice. They told him they were fugitives driven out by a king to die in the wilderness. Already many had fallen who would not rise again.

The elephant looked at them. They were weak. Without food and water they could never cross the mountains to the fertile, safe lands that lay beyond. He could direct them to his lake, but they were not strong enough to gather fruit in quantities. They must have sustaining food immediately.

"Have courage," he said to them, "in that direction you will find a lake of the clearest water (alas! his own dear, drowsy lake) and a little beyond there is a cliff at the foot of which you will find the body of an elephant who has recently fallen. Eat his flesh and you will have strength to reach the land beyond the mountains."

Then he saluted them and returned across the burning sands. Long before their feeble march had brought them to the lake and the cliff, he had thrown himself into the abyss

and had fallen, shining like a great moon sinking among clouds, and the spirits of the trees had thrown their flowers upon his body.

So the artist thought for a long time about the elephant's sagacity and dignity and kindness. Then he dipped a brush into spring water, touched it with ink, and drew an elephant.

No sooner was the elephant drawn, than Good Fortune came out of the artist's shadow and gazed round-eyed at the great creature standing upon the white silk. Then she looked at the artist. "I do not know what this being may be, master," she seemed to say, "but surely I am filled with awe from my whiskers to my tail."

Then again the artist sat on his mat and thought. This time he thought about horses. Although he had never ridden, he had often watched horses and admired their noble bearing, their shining eyes and curved necks. He liked the way they carried their tails like banners, and even in battle stepped carefully so as not to injure anyone who had fallen. He thought of Siddhartha's own horse, Kanthaka, white as snow, with a harness studded with jewels. He thought of how gentle and wild he was, how he had raced the horses of the other princes and beaten them, when the prince had won the princess Yosadhara. Then he imagined Kanthaka returning without his master to the palace, his beautiful head hanging low, and Siddhartha's apparel bound to his saddle.

Next the artist remembered the story of how once the spirit of Buddha himself had been born in the form of a horse, small, but of such fiery spirit that he became the war

steed of the King of Benares. Seven kings came to conquer his master and camped about his city. Then the chief knight of the besieged army was given the king's war horse to ride and, attacking each camp suddenly, managed to bring back as prisoners, one by one, six kings. In capturing the sixth king the horse was badly wounded. So the knight unloosened its mail to arm another horse for the seventh and last battle.

But the war horse found a voice.

"Our work will be undone," he cried. "Another horse cannot surprise the camp. Set me, sir, upon my feet, arm me once more. I will finish what I have begun!"

Weak with loss of blood, he charged the seventh camp, like a falcon striking down its prey, and the seventh king was captured. The King of Benares came, rejoicing, to meet them at the royal gate.

"Great king," said the war horse, "pardon your prisoners!" And then, before the servants could take off his armor, he fell dead, in the moment of victory, at his master's feet.

So, after long considering the courage and nobility of horses, the artist dipped a brush in spring water, touched it with ink, and drew a horse.

No sooner was the horse drawn than Good Fortune came out of the artist's shadow and regarded the picture for a long time. She looked at the artist with admiration.

"If a fly should light upon your horse, master," she seemed to say, "surely it would stamp and toss its head."

The Fourth Song of the Housekeeper

My master sits.
    All day he thinks.
He scarcely sees
    The tea he drinks.

He does not know
    That I am I.
He does not see
    Our cat pass by.

And yet our love
    Has its share, too,
In all the things
    His two hands do.

The food I cook
    In humbleness
Helps him a little
    Toward success.

The next day the artist again closed himself alone in the room overlooking the hydrangea bushes. Sitting on his mat, he decided that above the white horse's head a swan should be flying. He thought of the beauty of swans and the great beating of their wings, and of how they follow their kings on mighty flights along the roads of the air. He thought of how lightly they float in water like white lotuses.

Then he remembered a story from the boyhood of Prince Siddhartha, who was one day to become the Buddha. He was walking in the pleasure garden which his father had given him, watching swans fly over his head toward the Himalayas. Suddenly he heard the hiss of an arrow, and something swifter and more cruel than any bird drove past him through the air, and brought a wounded swan down at his feet. The young prince ran to the great bird and drew out the arrow. He tried the point against his own arm to find what this pain felt like which the bird had suffered. Then, as he was binding up the wound, attendants came to claim the swan as the spoil of the prince who was his cousin.

Siddhartha answered quietly: "My cousin attempted only to destroy the swan, I claim it since I have attempted to save it. Let the councilors of the king decide between us."

Then the quarrel of the princes was brought before the royal council and the swan was given to the boy who was to be the Buddha.

So, having reflected upon the dreamlike beauty of swans, the artist dipped his brush in spring water, touched it with ink, and drew a swan.

No sooner was the swan drawn than Good Fortune came out of the artist's shadow and looked at it well and long. Then she turned politely to the artist.

"There is wind under those wings, sir," she seemed to say. But there was just a hint in her manner to suggest that she thought his time might be better employed than in drawing birds.

The artist took food, and wandered for a few minutes in his little garden to refresh himself with the touch of the sun and the sound of the wind. He returned to his study by the hydrangeas and was about to think once more, when the housekeeper appeared at the door and bowed deeply.

"My master will weary himself into a fever," she said, politely but obstinately. "You have been Buddha and gods and horses, and that elephant curiosity, and snails and swans and—goodness only knows what else, all in a few days! It is more than flesh can bear! Your honored forehead looks like a scrubbing board and your eyes like candles. Now our neighbor has just sent his servant to invite you to take tea with him and I have said that you would be there directly."

Having spoken so firmly, she stood leaning forward with her hands on her knees, the picture of meekness.

"You may argue with a stone Jizo by the roadside, but you waste your breath if you argue with a woman!" cried the artist. He took a silver piece out of the priest's purse and gave it to her.

"Go, buy yourself some fine new material for a dress," he said. "It is a long time since you had anything pretty."

"A thousand thanks to Your Honor!" cried the housekeeper, much pleased, "and I will shut up Good Fortune in the bamboo basket while we are out of the house. You would think the picture was sugar, painted on cream, to watch her. I am afraid to leave her alone with it."

So it was not until the next morning that the artist was allowed to meditate in peace on the nature of buffalo. He thought how ugly they are, and how their horns curve like heavy moons on their foreheads. He thought how strong they are, and yet how willing to labor all day for their masters. He thought how fierce they are when attacked even by tigers, yet the village children ride on their backs as safe as birds on a twig.

The spirit of Buddha, himself, had not been too proud to

be born in the body of a buffalo. There were many stories of those days, but the one that the artist remembered best told of how the holy buffalo had belonged to a poor man. One day he spoke to his master in a human voice and said, "Lo, master, you are poor. I would willingly do something to help you. Go to the villagers and tell them that you have an animal here who can pull a hundred carts loaded with stones. They will bet that this is impossible and you will win a fortune."

But when the villagers had fastened the carts together and loaded them with heavy stones, and the great beast was harnessed to the first cart, the owner behaved after the manner of common drivers, brandishing his goad and cursing his animal to show off before the others. The buffalo would not move so much as an inch.

His owner, who had been poor before, was a great deal poorer after that. But one evening the buffalo said to him again:

"Why did you threaten me? Why did you curse me? Go to the villagers and bet again, twice as much this time. But treat me well."

Again the heavy carts were yoked together, again the villagers gathered, snickering behind their hands. But this time the poor man bathed his buffalo, and fed it sweet grain and put a garland of flowers about its neck. When the creature was fastened to the first of the hundred carts, his master stroked him and cried:

"Forward, my beauty! On! on! my treasure!" and the buffalo strained forward and pulled and stretched his muscles until they nearly cracked, and slowly, surely, the hundred carts moved forward.

Now when the artist had considered the honesty and self-respect of the buffalo, he dipped a brush in spring water, touched it with ink, and drew a buffalo.

No sooner was the buffalo drawn than Good Fortune came out of the artist's shadow and regarded it with the air of one who is trying to hide a certain dissatisfaction. Then she looked at the artist.

"Truly a buffalo!" she seemed to say, but something about the creature, perhaps its few hairs, must have tickled her sense of humor, for all at once she giggled. Quickly she lifted one little white paw and broke into a series of polite sneezes.

It may be that the artist was a little annoyed with Good Fortune, for, hardly knowing it himself, he had come to count on her praise. Yet it may have been pure chance which made him reflect next on dogs.

He thought of them as puppies, balls of down playing in the snow, with round black eyes and moist black muzzles. He thought of them as grown up, following their masters with lean strides or guarding lonely farms. He almost felt their warm tongues licking his hand, or saw them prance and roll to catch his eye.

"How faithful!" he thought, and tried to remember some tale of the spirit of Buddha in the form of a dog. But either he had forgotten it, or there was no such story. So he called to the housekeeper.

The old woman came in and bowed deeply to her master.

"Do sit down," said the artist, "and tell me any story about dogs that may happen to come into your head."

The old woman brought out a handkerchief and wiped her forehead. Then she sat down and bowed.

"In my village, sir," she began, "people say there once stood a ruined temple. After the priests left it, goblins and demons lived there. Every year they demanded the sacrifice of a maiden from the town, or they swore they would destroy every one. So on a certain day each year a girl was put into a basket and taken into the enclosure of the temple. She was never seen again. But at last the lot fell to a little girl who owned a dog named Shippeitaro. All the village put on white for mourning. All day the sound of weeping was heard in the street. But before evening a stranger came into the town. He was a wandering soldier. The night before he had slept in a ruined temple."

"The temple of the goblins?" asked the artist.

"Yes, master," said the old woman, "it was the same temple. The soldier had been wakened in the night by a great

racket. A voice over his head was saying, 'But never let Shippeitaro know—Shippeitaro would ruin everything.'

"When the soldier told his story, Shippeitaro became greatly excited. He ran to the basket, wagging his tail, and clawed at its side.

" 'Let him be taken to the temple in place of his mistress,' said the soldier, and Shippeitaro leaped, of his own free will, into the basket and was carried through the gathering darkness to the temple courtyard. Then the bearers hurried away, but the soldier hid himself and waited.

"At midnight he heard the most terrible yowlings approaching. They were enough to freeze the blood cold in one's veins. He peered out and saw a troupe of goblins prying off the lid of the basket. But instead of a frightened girl, out jumped Shippeitaro and sprang at the leader's throat. The other goblins fled and they have never been seen or heard of since.

"So the good dog Shippeitaro saved not only his mistress but all the village."

The artist thanked the old woman for her story. Good Fortune, who had found a mat to sit on, had been listening to the story as attentively as her master.

"What form had these goblins?" asked the artist.

"Cats," answered the housekeeper, almost in a whisper, hoping that Good Fortune would not hear. But Good Fortune did hear. With a sad look at the old woman, she rose and walked out of the room.

The artist, after reflecting upon the fidelity of dogs, dipped a brush in spring water, touched it with ink, and drew a dog.

Good Fortune did not come back all day to look at it.

The Fifth Song of the Housekeeper

Dear pussy, you are white as milk,
Your mouth's a blossom, your coat's silk—
What most distinguished family tree
Produced so great a rarity?

Dear pussy, you are soft and sweet;
You are too holy to touch meat—
What most distinguished family tree
Produced so great a rarity?

Dear pussy, you must never think
I thought *you* kin to cats like ink—
For goblin beasts could never be
Produced by such a family tree!
By such a lovely family tree!

The next day when the artist seated himself upon his mat
there was no Good Fortune sitting nearby but discreetly
out of the way. For a few minutes he could not help thinking of his little three-colored cat, but soon he was able to
turn his mind to deer. He must paint the animals who came
to bid farewell to the Buddha, and he knew the cat was not
among them.

At first his thought was sad, but little by little he imagined a forest about him, dappled with light and shade, and
he himself was a deer, setting small hoofs like ebony among
the leaves, making no sound, listening with head raised high
under its fairy branching of horns. A herd of deer followed
him, the young males and the does and the fawns. He led
them to secret pastures. At each water hole his wide nos-
trils scented the wind for danger before the others came to

drink. If an enemy appeared, he guarded the flight of the herd. His sides were set with spots like jewels; his horns were more beautiful than temple candlesticks; his eyes were shy and wild.

Slowly, while the artist wandered through imaginary forests as a deer, he felt growing within him the spirit of the Buddha, and he knew that he was the Banyan deer. Then it seemed to him that he and his herd had been driven into a great enclosure with another herd of deer, whose leader was almost as beautiful as he. His heart beat like thunder between his ribs and a darkness came before his eyes, but his fear was for the sake of his herd. Then there came a king into the enclosure to look at the deer.

"The leaders are too beautiful to die," he said to his huntsman. "I grant them their lives. But of the others, see that you bring one each day to the palace for my banquets."

Then the Banyan deer, who was filled with the spirit of Buddha, said to all the deer:

"If we are hunted, many deer will be hurt each day. Let us meet this with fortitude and let a lot be drawn. Let the deer to whom it falls die voluntarily for the good of the herd."

Now one day the lot fell to a doe whose fawn had not yet been born. It happened that she belonged to the other herd. She went to the leader and begged that she might live until the fawn was born.

"We can make no exceptions," said he sadly.

But when in despair she went to the Banyan deer, he sent her back comforted.

"I will take your place," he said.

The artist, who in his mind was living the life of the deer, felt how his tenderness for the doe and the unborn fawn overcame his terror and led him gladly to the huntsman. But when the man saw that it was the great leader of the deer, himself, who had come, he sent for the king.

"Did I not grant you your life?" asked the king, surprised.

Then the Banyan deer found a human voice to answer.

"O king!" he said, "the lot had fallen upon a doe with an unborn fawn. I could not ask another to take her place."

Then the king, pleased by the deer's generosity, granted their lives both to him and to the doe.

Still the Banyan deer was not satisfied, but pled for his people.

"But the others, O king?" he asked.

"They, too, shall live," said the king.

"There are the deer outside the palings," went on the Banyan deer.

"They shall not be troubled," replied the king.

"O king," continued the deer, who, having always lived in danger, pitied all creatures in the same case, "what shall other four-footed creatures do?"

And the king was so moved by the deer's intended sacrifice that he, too, felt tenderly toward the world.

"They shall have no reason for fear," he answered.

Then the deer interceded for the birds and even for the fish, and when their safety was promised, he blessed the king with a great blessing.

The artist, whose heart had seemed torn with timidity and gentle courage while he imagined himself the Banyan

deer, quickly caught up a brush, dipped it in spring water, touched it with ink, and drew a deer.

No sooner was the deer drawn than Good Fortune came out unexpectedly from the artist's shadow (she had entered so quietly he had never noticed) and looked long at the picture.

"Miaou," she said, sadly turning to the artist. "Is there no room for me among the other animals, master?" she seemed to ask.

After that the artist drew many creatures. In each of them the spirit of the Buddha had at one time lived, or it had rendered service to him when he was a prince on earth. There were the woodpecker, and the hare who jumped into the frying pan of the beggar, and the lion who saved the young hawks, and the goose who gave his golden feathers to the old woman, and the wise little goat who outwitted the wolves, and many others.

He drew a monkey, too, remembering how when the spirit of Buddha lived in an ape, a man, wandering in the jungle, had fallen into a deep pit. Then the great ape, having heard his groans, found a voice to reassure him. He climbed down into the pit, and, fastening a stone to his back, tested his strength to make sure that he could climb out once more, carrying the man. At last, having succeeded, the ape was so exhausted that he knew he must sleep or he would die. So he begged the man to watch by him while he slept. But as the man watched, evil thoughts came into his mind.

"If I only had meat to eat, I should easily be strong enough to find my way home," he thought.

Forgetting gratitude, he picked up a large stone and

struck the monkey on the head. But the blow of his weak arm had little strength. The ape started up and saw that it was the man whom he had saved who had tried to kill him. Surprise and sorrow filled him at such ingratitude. Nevertheless, he led the man out of the forest to the edge of the fields and bade him farewell, showing compassion even to his betrayer.

The artist remembered also how the monkeys had brought fruit to the Buddha, when he sat in meditation in the forest, and coaxed him to eat with their droll ways.

So having meditated upon the monkey, the artist dipped a brush in spring water, touched it with ink, and drew a monkey.

And as the painting of each animal was finished, Good Fortune came to look at it, and with each new drawing she seemed sadder and pulled with her little white paw at the sleeve of her master, looking up all the time into his face.

The Sixth Song of the Housekeeper

She's sure to starve,
    She *won't* grow fat,
No dinner tempts
    Our little cat!

All day I follow,
    All day I cry,
"Come, pussy, come, pussy,"
    As she goes by.

But she will starve,
    She *won't* grow fat,
It's always that painting
    She's looking at.

All day I grieve
    To hear her cry,
"Miaou, miaou,"
    As I go by!

One day the artist sat on his mat and his mind wrestled with a more difficult problem than any that had come up before. The gentleness of the snail, the noble strength and wisdom of the elephant, the courage of the horse, the beauty of the wild swan, the willing endurance of the buffalo, the serviceableness of the dog and the generosity of the deer all made it easy to see how they might have served the Buddha, or even have been used by his spirit as temporary dwelling places. So, also, with the woodpecker, the hare, the goose, the little goat and the ape, all were harmless creatures; and even the lion killed only to appease his hunger, and took no joy in the killing.

But the artist knew that the tiger, too, had come to bid farewell to the Buddha, and he, too, had received the master's blessing. How could that be? He thought of the fierceness and cruelty of tigers, he imagined them lying in the striped shadows of the jungle, with their eyes of fire. They

were the danger by the water hole; the killers among the reeds. Now and then, one came to the villages and carried away some woman on her way to the well. Or again one killed a man at work in a field, or carried away a child playing in the dust outside the door of his own house.

What was there in such a creature that the Buddha could bless?

Long and long the artist pondered, sitting in silence, and at last he remembered how devoted a tiger was to his own mate and cubs, and how he would face any odds if these were in danger. He thought: "It may be that this is the narrow pathway by which the tiger reaches to the Buddha. It may be that there is a fierceness in love, and love in fierceness."

So, having opened his mind to the thought of love, even in a tiger, the artist remembered something that he had forgotten until then. Before his mind came a vision of how

Siddhartha had won his bride. In open contest with the other princes, he who was to be the Buddha had drawn the bow no other hand could draw, had ridden the horse no other man could ride and had shown a skill and strength as a swordsman that none of the others could equal. Watching from her golden palanquin sat the princess, Yosadhara, her face hidden behind a veil of striped black and gold.

Now at last came the victor's reward. Yosadhara's father led Siddhartha to his daughter's side and it was then he whispered, "By your veil I know that you remember how once, in another life, you were a tigress, and I was the tiger who won you in open combat against all the others."

So, among many forms, the Buddha had deigned to take the form of a tiger, as if to prove that even in such a savage life there may be something of greatness. And having once more meditated, and now willingly, upon this beautiful creature, sinister but capable of any burning sacrifice, the artist dipped his brush in spring water, touched it with ink, and drew a tiger.

Good Fortune came out from his shadow. When she saw the tiger she trembled all over, from her thistle-down whiskers to her little tail, and looked at the artist.

"If the tiger can come to bid farewell to Buddha," she seemed to say, "surely the cat, who is little and often so gentle, may come, O master? Surely, surely, you will next paint the cat among the animals who were blessed by the Holy One as he died?"

The artist was much distressed.

"Good Fortune," he said, gently taking her into his arms, "I would gladly paint the cat if I could. But all people know

that cats, though lovely, are usually proud and self-satisfied. Alone among the animals, the cat refused to accept the teachings of Buddha. She alone, of all creatures, was not blessed by him. It is perhaps in grief that she too often consorts with goblins."

Then Good Fortune laid her little round head against his breast and mewed and mewed like a crying child. He comforted her as well as he could and called for the housekeeper.

"Buy her a fine fish all for herself," he said to the old woman. "And do not let her come here again until the picture is gone. She will break both our hearts."

"Ah, I was afraid she meant to do the painting a harm," said the old woman anxiously. For she felt very responsible for having brought the cat home against her master's will, now that their fortunes hung on this painting for the temple.

"It is not that," said the artist, and he returned to his thoughts. How tired, how worn he looked, and yet how beautiful! His picture was almost finished. He had imagined every life. There lay the great figure of the dying Buddha, royal, weary, compassionate. There assembled gods and men; and there were the animals. The scroll of silk seemed scarcely large enough to hold all those varied lives, all that gathering of devotion about the welling-up of love.

But something was excluded. From the kitchen he heard a faint mewing, and the housekeeper's voice in vain urging Good Fortune to eat. The artist imagined how his little cat felt, so gentle, so sweet, but cursed forever. All the other animals might receive the Buddha's blessing and go to heaven, but the little cat heard the doors of Nirvana closed before her. Tears came to his eyes.

"I cannot be so hard-hearted," he said. "If the priests wish to refuse the picture as inaccurate, let them do so. I can starve."

He took up his best brush, dipped it in spring water, touched it with ink, and, last of all the animals, *drew a cat*.

Then he called the housekeeper.

"Let Good Fortune come in," he said. "Perhaps I have ruined us, but I can at least make her happy."

In came Good Fortune, the moment that the door was slid open. She ran to the picture, and looked and looked, as though she could never look enough. Then she gazed at the artist with all her gratitude in her eyes. And then Good Fortune fell dead, too happy to live another minute.

The Seventh Song of the Housekeeper

I can't believe it—
  (And how I've cried)
But out of pure joy
  Good Fortune died.

At the foot of her grave
  Lie a flower and a shell,
In the peach tree near by
  Hangs a little bell,

A little old bell
  With a sweet cracked voice,
When a wind passes by
  It sings, "Rejoice!"

"Rejoice!" it sings
  Through the gardenside,
"For out of pure joy
  Good Fortune died!"

The next morning, hearing that the picture was finished, the priest came to see it. After the first greetings, the artist led him in to look at the painting. The priest gazed long.

"How it shines," he said softly.

Then his face hardened.

"But what is that animal whom you have painted last of all?" he asked.

"It is a cat," said the painter, and his heart felt heavy with despair.

"Do you not know," asked the priest sternly, "that the cat rebelled against our Lord Buddha, and did not receive his blessing and cannot enter heaven?"

"Yes, I knew," said the artist.

"Each person must suffer the consequences of his own acts," said the priest. "The cat must suffer from her obstinacy and you from yours. As one can never erase work once done, I will take the painting and tomorrow officially burn it. Some other artist's picture must hang in our temple."

All day the housekeeper wept in the kitchen, for in bringing the little cat home she had, after all, ruined her master.

All day the artist sat in the room beside the hydrangeas and thought. His painting was gone and with it that part of his life which he had put into it. Tomorrow the priests would harshly burn it in the courtyard of the temple. Less than ever would any one come to him now. He was ruined and all his hopes gone. But he did not regret what he had done. For so many days had he lived in the thought of love and the examples of sacrifice, that it did not seem too hard to suffer for Good Fortune's great moment of happiness.

All night he sat in the darkness open-eyed with his thoughts. The old woman dared not interrupt. He saw the pale light enter through the blinds and heard the dawn wind in the hydrangea bushes. An hour later, he heard the noise of people running toward his house. The priests of the temple surrounded him; the head priest pulled at his sleeve.

"Come! Come!" they kept crying. "Come, sir! It is a miracle! Oh, the compassion of Buddha! Oh, the mercy of the Holy One!"

Dazed and breathless, the artist followed them, seeing nothing of the village or the road to the temple. He heard happy voices in his ears, he caught a glimpse of his old housekeeper with her sash askew, and a crowd of open-mouthed neighbors. All together they poured into the temple. There hung his picture with incense and candles burning before it. It was as he had remembered it, but, no!——

The artist sank down to his knees with a cry:

"Oh, the Compassionate One!" For where the last animal

had stood was now only white silk that seemed never to have felt the touch of ink; and the great Buddha, the Buddha whom he had painted reclining with hands folded upon his breast, had stretched out an arm in blessing, and under the holy hand knelt the figure of a tiny cat, with pretty white head bowed in happy adoration.

The Eighth Song of the Housekeeper

This is too great a mystery
  For me to comprehend:
The mercy of the Buddha
  Has no end.
This is too beautiful a thing
  To understand:
His garments touch the furthest
  Grain of sand.